Nothing
Said

Nothing Said

L. M. Boston

ILLUSTRATED BY
PETER BOSTON

Harcourt Brace Jovanovich, Inc.
New York

Copyright © 1971 by Lucy Maria Boston

FIRST AMERICAN EDITION

A B C D E F G H I J
Hardbound edition ISBN 0-15-257580-4
Library edition ISBN 0-15-257581-2
Library of Congress Catalog Card Number: 70-137756

PRINTED IN THE UNITED STATES OF AMERICA

The lines of poetry on page 25 are from "Overheard on a Saltmarsh" by Harold Monro and are quoted from *Collected Poems* by Harold Monro by permission of the publisher, Gerald Duckworth & Co., Ltd.

To *Judy Taylor*
with love

"I DON'T WANT TO GO TO AUNT MAUD," said Libby desperately. "I don't like her."

"Hush!" said her mother. "You mustn't say that."

"I don't like her. And I hate those cousins. I won't go." She looked flushed and woebegone, because what can you do when your parents say you must?

"You know Daddy and I are obliged to go to this conference. We can't help it, and until school begins again, you must be somewhere."

It was the summer half term—a whole week in

June. To waste it was more than Libby could bear.

"She could stay with me," said Julia. "It is a long way to go, but it would be a change for her. My brother is away and I am alone. I would like to have her."

"Could I really?" said Libby, overawed by the idea.

Julia was a tall young woman with remarkably beautiful eyes and a personality not to be trifled with. Except that you couldn't help liking her, it was difficult to know anything about her. She was a painter who once had taught at Libby's school. She was casually kind, as between equals, and she never interfered, but what opinion she had of you, if you could ever know it, was important.

"Would you like to come with me?" she now asked.

"Yes. I would."

"Then I can take you back in my car this afternoon. There will be no other children, but I live by a river, and that is very good company. And I have a dog."

The parents agreed, and when Libby had said good-bye to them, she went off in the car with Julia, excited to be in such unexpected grown-up company and to be going to a new place.

It was a long journey. Before they even got clear of London's suburbs, Libby was lolling and kicking her heels. Then came the main road, and that was worse, for it was all the same as far as one could see or think—the same signs, the same banks, the same bridges and roundabouts, the same smell, even the same speed. What she could see of fields and hedges looked tired and waste, so that however little she enjoyed being whisked through it, there was nowhere where she longed to stop. The thrill of going somewhere new gave way to a longing to have arrived. At last they were on smaller roads, going up and down hill and winding about, but by that time it was dark. She could no longer see out, but through the open window came a different kind of air, a sweet softness of earth scents released at night. The headlights of an approaching car made her close her eyes, and without knowing it she fell deeply asleep against Julia's shoulder.

When the car finally stopped, she was too sleepy to take anything in. She let herself be put to bed and tucked up, and just slept on.

When Libby woke in the morning, she was surprised to find she was not in the car, but in a small four-poster. It was as if something very queer had happened. She lay still for a while looking at the roof and curtains of the bed. They were made of printed linen, which had a pattern of tree trunks and leaves. When the curtains swayed in the moving air, the trees swayed and the leaves rippled. Once she thought she saw a girl's face look out from the trees. Libby caught hold of the stuff and held it out tight and straight. There was no face in the pattern. But what a lovely

place to lie in! One could think a lot of things in this bed. Then she remembered that she did not know what kind of place she had come to.

She jumped out of her curtains into a room hardly bigger than the four-poster and ran to the open French window, curtained down to the ground with the same tree-patterned stuff. She found with surprise that she was on the ground floor, looking out under the branches of splendid trees. They stood in grassland that sloped upward to a thick wood. Behind that could be seen more woods on distant hills. There was not a house in sight nor any sound of traffic, but a continuous and enticing sound of running water and the song of hundreds of birds. The air was soft and spicy. She wanted to drink it.

On the grass was a fox terrier. He saw her at the window and barked. Libby began to get dressed, and in a minute the dog had come in. He was impatient. He brought her a shoe before she was ready for it, barked while she brushed her hair, and ran to the door and back. Finally he brought her a glove as if to say, "Now we are going out," then ran before her down the passage.

At home Libby lived in a new house. When you went in at the door, you could see all there was. The bottom room was kitchen, dining, and living room all in one. The open stairs went out of it, and you could see a bedroom above. In fact, you didn't even have to go in. You could see everything from the street, through the big windows.

Julia's house was very old, full of odd corners and recesses, with doors everywhere of different sizes. Without opening one it was impossible to guess if it would lead to another room, a cupboard, a passage, or stairs. Everywhere was so full of pictures and bookshelves and oddments that there wouldn't have been room for one thing more.

Now the dog led Libby to the breakfast room, which she never could have found by herself. The sun was shining through the pleasantly crooked sash window, making every object lively. Each picture or ornament or rug seemed to have a mysterious life of its own. She did not know what to look at first.

Julia was putting the breakfast on a table by the window. This was on the other side of the house, looking downhill, across a garden tumbling with happy casual flowers. At the lowest end was a bank, walled along the top, beyond which could be heard the river.

"Come along, Libby," said Julia. "You are in good time. You must have slept well. Do you remember being put to bed?"

"No, I don't. And when I woke up, I thought the bed was the car gone wrong. It was such a surprise! Like a nice dream. Then I got up to see where I had come to, and your dog was outside. He seemed to be waiting for me."

"He helped me to put you to bed last night."

"How did he help? He can't undo buttons."

"No, he can't. But I gave him your shoes, and he

put them away somewhere. Under the carpet, I think. Did you have to hunt for them?"

"He brought them to me before I missed them."

"Clever Cobweb! He's called Cobweb because his whiskers are so soft and cobwebby."

Cobweb's tail was banging against the table leg. Libby put a hand down to feel his whiskers and laughed.

"He led me upstairs and then down again. I saw your river from the staircase window."

"*My* river! That does sound grand. I don't think it belongs to anybody. It's just itself. It is called the Babble."

"It's a pity you can't see it from here. That walled bank at the end of the garden is in the way."

"Behind that wall is the footpath. It has to be raised like that because the river sometimes floods."

"Then without a bank your garden would get flooded."

"It does anyway. That's why there is that causeway down the garden to the river. It used to be stepping stones across the marsh. They must have drawn their water from the river before there was a well. Then stone slabs were put across the top to make a kind of bridge or viaduct. You see, the river Babble long ago was much bigger. All my garden is on the old riverbed. If you dig down a little way, you soon come to pebbles, just like the bottom of the river now. When the water rises, it finds its way through the gravel underneath the bank and fills up its old bed again. It happens most winters, but the house is high enough up to stand clear. If you have finished breakfast, you cán take Cobweb to the river for a walk. He'll show you round."

Cobweb was more than delighted. He knew she was a visitor, and so he was showing off. He ran rings round her as they went down the garden, but was waiting for her by the gate, which he unlatched with a masterly paw. He did allow a second for her to go through, but then pushed past her legs and was first again at the river's edge.

Libby followed him slowly because she was gasping with surprise. How could one ever guess that right away from towns and main roads the country was like this? The air was as scented as any bunch of flowers. The wind moved it about and continually brought it fresh again. No wonder Cobweb wiggled his nose. What most surprised Libby was that everything looked new. The sky looked new. The light was so clean that every detail of the opposite side of the valley was clear and precise. The trees had never been lopped or deformed, but each spread to the ideal shape it needed to be, every little twig feeling its place in the pattern. They looked as much alive as the birds. The hedges had never had dust on the leaves or wastepaper on the roots. They seemed to be sheltered, privileged places where anything could grow if it could get in, foxgloves and honeysuckle, wild roses, hops, primroses and ferns. The footpath was narrow and hardly trodden. It could have been a natural break in

the spread of plants. If bracken grew alongside, its neck was not broken by passing bicycles, but arched out like the vaulting of a miniature green cathedral; if harebells grew, their threadlike stalks were unlikely ever to be trodden on, and all the host of pretty seeding grasses simply lived there safely. At first Libby only saw details, examining all the richness, and then, harder to take in, the great expanse—how much of this paradise there was. A few farmhouses, scattered over the hillsides, were far enough away to underline the solitude.

Most wonderful of all, and running through the whole of it, filling it with thrilling sound, was the Babble. It was the kind of river that has gravel and pebbles at each side and flows round and over big stones in the center. Over each smooth boulder it made a waterfall, and under each waterfall there was an eddy with bubbles circling round and round. Little rapids escaped from the eddies in any direction they could find and hurried along to the next holdup. The whole stream flashed in the sun and chattered like a swarm of children. Swallows circled and dipped to the surface, or sat on an overhanging branch to sing. Their song was a non-stop ripple, as if they had learned it from the river.

Cobweb was at the edge, digging for stones. It had to be a stone he liked, and he was very choosy. Finally he brought out a round pinkish one that just fitted his mouth open to its widest. He dropped it at Libby's feet and crouched in front of her ready to dash

in any direction. Libby threw it back into the water, where it made a musical, skidding plop. In went Cobweb, his back legs straddling on a boulder while he plunged his head and shoulders down. She wondered how he could keep his head under for so long, seeing that he must sniff to recognize the stone and open his mouth to its widest to bring it back. He was very determined, and if he came up gasping now and then with his eyebrows dripping over his eyes, he always brought the right one.

The river was shallow, but here and there were deeper pools hollowed out by the current, where, if she threw so far, the stone fell with quite a different sound, where Cobweb would never go, but just stood barking. Then he would choose another stone for himself, and so the game could have gone on a long time, but the sun suddenly vanished behind gathering clouds, and there was a sharp dash of rain.

Libby turned back toward the house, followed by Cobweb carrying his stone. It was too heavy for him, and she could see his neck muscles tensed with the strain, but he would not let her have it, even if he had to drop it for a rest. At last he placed it by the front porch and wagged at Julia, who had come out to meet them.

"Thank you, Cobweb! Good dog!" she said. "You see, Libby, I am making a border of stones round this pansy bed. Cobweb brings them for me, all just about the same size, mouth-measured."

Julia placed the stone carefully in its place. "No,

Cobweb, don't dig it up again. It stays there now.
Come and be dried. Come in, you too, Libby, and wait
till it stops raining." As she spoke, there was a clap of
thunder, and the rain came down as if a hole had been
torn in the sky. From inside the house you would have
thought someone was playing a hosepipe against the
windows. Very soon all the gutters were overflowing.

Now was the time to explore the house, which Libby longed to do. It was small but complicated. She found four staircases, two of beautifully polished wood with fat round banisters and easy treads, one of stone going from the kitchen to a storeroom, one a corkscrew going to the smallest bedrooms, and lots of little ups and downs. Landings and passages ran this way and that, all hung with pictures and clocks and mirrors and masks and peacocks' feathers. Cobweb ran before her, jumping up onto every window seat to look out—always expecting excitements—or showing her which door she was to open next. Obviously he found the house intensely interesting and liked some places better than others. When she put her hand on the doorknob of one of the bedrooms, Cobweb stiffened and quivered like a dog who sees a cat through the window, and as she turned the knob, he gave the kind of ecstasy moan of one who is about to be allowed to chase it. Libby opened the door slowly, and he shot in, to bark defiantly at a large picture hanging on the opposite wall. It showed a lot of young girls, quite bare, bathing in a pool in some very secret place. They had yards and yards of wet hair floating in the water round their shoulders and were all lifting their arms toward a handsome boy who was bending down on the bank. One of the girls held him by the arm. She wore a crown of water lilies. They were all smiling and coaxing. On the frame it said *Hylas and the Nymphs*. Libby thought it a very beautiful picture and wished it hung in her room, but Cobweb shouted at it and nudged her shin with his muzzle, as if he thought she ought to bark, too. She thought he was making too much noise, so she dragged him out of the room and shut the door. At this he left her for the first time and went helter-skelter downstairs. Through the rain-dashed window Libby watched him cross the garden toward the river, where he gave a couple of barks, then, as if he had done what he considered fit and proper, he turned back and shook the rain off his coat as much as he could—he shook so hard that he shook his front legs off the ground—then trotted back to the house.

Libby rubbed him dry again and went to look for Julia.

"There's a picture upstairs called something and the Nymphs. I like it specially, but Cobweb barks at it. Is the boy someone he doesn't like?"

"I don't think it's the boy. Hylas he was called. But Cobweb never met him."

"The girls then? What are nymphs?"

"They are river spirits. The picture is about a well-known story. Hylas went to fetch water from the river. It was summer, and at the place where he went every day the water now was too shallow to reach the lip of his pitcher, so he went along the bank looking for somewhere deeper. He came at last to a beautiful pool, edged with wild flowers and sur-rounded by trees, very secret and silent, and, he

thought, holy, or at least in some way frightening. The water was clear and tempting. He leaned over the edge to lower his pitcher, and the nymphs looking up from the bottom saw his face looking down. At once they wanted to keep him for themselves. They rose up to the surface and surrounded him, and there they beguiled him with their wonderful grace and the streams of their hair coiling and uncoiling on the stirred water. So he crouched there and bent lower, till one of them put her arms round his neck, and they took him down to the bottom."

"Then did he live there with the nymphs?"

"People who like all stories to end happily say so. But I think he just got drowned. And then they sang a sad song and went to look for something else. Nymphs are not very trustworthy."

"But how could Cobweb know the story? He's very intelligent, but can you tell him stories?"

"I have no idea how much Cobweb knows or hears, but I should think he only knows what he has met. But he may meet things we don't know about. When he's alone in the garden at night, for instance. Certainly the picture seems to remind him of something he doesn't trust."

"Are there pools like that in this river?"

"Oh yes. There's a deep one just beside the footpath, where that huge elm tree leans over."

"It's not very private for nymphs by a footpath."

"Hardly anybody uses it but me and an occasional fisherman. It's a shortcut between two villages. There are weeks when nobody goes along. There are moonlight nights and long early mornings, and wet days, too, like today. Nothing's so private as rain in the country. So you see, there's nothing to stop you imagining anything you like."

Libby looked out of the window. The cloud roof was only just above the trees, and the drenched emerald green of the lawn and the fresh summer leaves reflected up onto the clouds and made them greenish too. The air itself seemed green. Veils of rain moved across the garden, and on the fingertips of branches big emerald drops formed and fell and broke in sparkles. Among them the wagtails ran, taking it over as fairyland, and a big green woodpecker feeding on the lawn flew away with a shout of weird laughter. When rain settles in, secret things come out. The one really surprising thing to have seen out there would have been a human being.

Libby turned to Julia. "This morning, when Cobweb was digging for stones, I was choosing pebbles. I found this. Look, it's pretty." She put in Julia's hand a marble-sized transparent green bead. "Somebody's thread must have broken. Was it yours?"

Julia shook her head. Libby went on. "I wish I could find the others, but I suppose they have gone rolling down the river, over the little waterfalls—like a marble run."

Julia was still looking at the bead, smiling. "It reminds me," she said, "of a poem I read when I was your age.

"Nymph, nymph, what are your beads?
Green glass, goblin. Why do you stare at them?
Give them me.
         No.
Give them me. Give them me.
             No.
Then I will howl all night in the reeds,
Lie in the mud and howl for them.
Goblin, why do you love them so?

      . . .

Give me your beads, I want them.
           No.
I will howl in a deep lagoon
For your green glass beads, I love them so.
Give them me. Give them.
       No."

Silence fell between them. Libby dared not ask what she wanted to know. Instead she said, "May I keep it, or must I put it back?"

"Of course you can keep it. I will put a silk thread through it, and you can wear it round your neck and play at being a nymph in your bath. Hand me my sewing basket, please. There you are." The bead was hung round Libby's neck.

"Do you have goblins?" she asked.

"Are you afraid one will try to snatch it off you

in the night? You can trust Cobweb to keep them away. How often I've seen him chase them up trees, and how they squawked and gabbled!"

Libby didn't know whether to believe her or not.

Cobweb was the life of the house. He could play many games—Hide-and-Seek, Hunt the Slipper, Dressing-up, Catch—and was a willing fielder for Ninepins. He insisted on being kept amused.

By evening it was still raining heavily, if anything even more relentlessly. Clouds lay over the hills like wet black eiderdowns, while the valley lying between was streaked with vertical downpourings.

Cobweb was put outside, but he did not go beyond the veranda. He barked, turning his head north, south, east, and west, as if to inform anything within earshot—cottagers, owls, badgers, foxes, cats, and whatever else—that he was there on his own ground. Only an owl answered him. Then he came in and settled down in his basket.

Libby lay in her bed, surrounded, if she took her flashlight from under her pillow, by a pattern of trunks and leaves. It was almost like a tree house within a tree house. She listened to the rain, trying to imagine she was a bird. She could hear it on the big trees outside her window, falling in a steady deluge, but it was much noisier and livelier on the house, drumming on the different slopes of the roof, soft on thatch, loud on slate, gurgling in the gutters, running in streams from the spouts, overflowing in waterfalls onto the roof of the veranda, dropping like little bombs off the edge into the water butt. Behind all these interesting sounds was the river chattering away through the night, telling stories to dream about.

When Libby woke in the morning, these watery noises were still going on, but the river was no longer chattering. It was laying down the law angrily, and nothing was going to stand in its way. Through every window she heard it as she came downstairs from the bathroom.

"Come and look at the river," said Julia. "You won't recognize it."

In boots and mackintoshes they crossed the sopping grass and mounted the bank. Cobweb sniffed the wider area of wet air with suspicion.

The shingle on either side of the stream had vanished under water. The Babble, brown with sand and clay and twice as wide, was roaring along in rapids and spurts of foam. It was well below the top of the bank, but Julia said there was a lot more water to come. There had been cloudbursts on the hills from which the Babble sprang. "A flood in summer will be new to me, but we might get one if this rain goes on."

"Don't you mind? Is it frightening?"

"No. It will be interesting."

On the river side of the path grew the magnificent tree of which Julia had spoken earlier. Its trunk was almost as wide and rutted as a cart track. It had come with wind and weather to lean far out over the

water, its furrowed slope not steeper than Cobweb could scramble. He went up now as far as the first big branch.

"He'll fall in," gasped Libby in an agony.

"No, he won't fall. That tree is quite a favorite of his. Of course, he can't climb like a cat. I expect he wishes he could."

Cobweb lay down in the angle of the branch and rubbed his whiskers lovingly on the bark. Then he inspected the view from up there, especially downward where the deep water eddied. He came down the wet, slippery trunk with care but also with some bravado. Julia and Libby went in to breakfast, glad to take off their streaming rain clothes.

Breakfast time is good for looking at things with a fresh eye. In this room where there were so many things to look at, some were either not seen at first or not taken in. Julia, for instance, collected china ornaments, particularly the sort that have figures, or houses to be lit up with night lights. On the mantelpiece in front of Libby where she sat, there was such a house at one end and a little white chapel called Bethel at the other. In between were two pieces that now caught her eye. They both showed a gnarled tree trunk with sprays of china leaves molded and stuck on and colored green and brown. The trunks of the trees were split open, and out of each came the thigh and the upper part of a girl's body, dusky skinned, half covered with her long green hair.

Libby pointed to them. "On my bed curtains I thought I saw a face like that. But I must have been

dreaming because it wasn't there really. What are they?"

Julia leaned back to pick them off the mantel-piece. She put them on the table in front of Libby.

"Allow me to introduce you. Dryads—Libby, Libby—Dryads."

Libby handled them with care and pleasure while Cobweb looked on, grinning. "They are nice," she said. "What are dryads?"

"They are tree spirits and live in trees."

"Does every tree have one?"

"Oh, I think that would be overcrowding. Not every tree has a nightingale. Some things are rare. I can't see them living in London squares or in avenues along main roads or in municipal parks. But in the country you can enjoy such ideas, and in real country you can't stop yourself imagining all kinds of wonders, to explain why the country is so wonderful it-self."

"This is real country," said Libby with certainty.

"As real as anything that's left. If we go on like this building roads and houses and factories and airfields, someday, somewhere, there will be the very last butterfly or the very last dryad."

"No," said Libby. "No, no."

Cobweb jumped onto her knees to comfort her, and Julia, seeing that she had grieved her, carried on the conversation from a pleasanter point of view.

"One of my visitors calls your room the Dryad Room because it looks into the branches of big trees. She is a very old lady, and when she was young, she lived in one of those great houses that had armies of servants and perhaps fifty or more bedrooms. They naturally had names—the Blue Room, the Lilac Room, the Paneled Room, Queen Elizabeth's Room, the Old Duke's Room. You can imagine it was much easier than telling the housemaid to prepare the fifth room on the second floor of the north side of the east wing and also the seventh on the first floor of the William and Mary block on the courtyard side."

"Are dryads untrustworthy, like nymphs?"

"Not at all. They are much too shy."

"Did the old lady ever see a dryad in those trees?"

"She is rather a mysterious old lady. She never said she had."

"I shall," said Libby. Cobweb nudged her under her chin with his muzzle. "Shan't I?" she answered him fondly.

After breakfast they all went off in the car to the nearest village to lay in supplies in case the floods came up and cut off the road. Libby hoped the floods would come and last for weeks, so that she could not go back to school. But when they came back, with the car swishing up waves of mud and the windows covered with splash, it had stopped raining.

As soon as the engine was switched off, they heard the river. They went straight to the bank to see how it was getting on. It could no longer be called the Babble. No boulders showed above its waters, no waterfalls, no wandering swirls, but a great purposeful rush of deep water making for the sea. Only here and there on the surface was a smooth swelling which showed that the biggest boulders were there underneath. There was no laughing chatter now, but a shrill hissing of tearing ripples and at the sides a slapping, sucking, swallowing. Over all hung an oppressive tumult which seemed to have followed it from higher upstream or to be escaping from the churning stones in its bed—something that was more felt than heard. At the side of the bank the roots of the tree had been licked bare.

Cobweb was standing on three legs looking uncertainly at a crack in the footpath beside his favorite tree. He sidestepped it and cocked his ears. Julia came to examine it.

"It looks as if the tree is dragging its anchor. If we got a gale now, it would be toppled over. It has all the weight of its leaves on it. I should hate to lose it."

As she spoke, the sun came out, as suddenly as thirty-six hours ago it had gone in.

"Ah, that's better. Let's hope there is no wind, and when the water goes down, the tree will grow new roots and take firm hold again."

They crossed the grass going back to the house and could feel that though it had been rained on so much, the real wet was coming up from below. It squirted round their boots.

"I think I can promise you that you can paddle in the garden this afternoon. The river is finding its way to its old bed."

After lunch in the warm sun, Libby came out in

bare feet to test the lawns. Here and there little pools were forming; it was like paddling on the seashore when the tide is coming in. Pools grow wider and deeper till they join up with their neighbors. From many little hidden springs pushing up through the turf, the lawns were gradually covered with distilled water, quite unlike the turbulent river from which it had come. It was cleansed with its slow sieving through the gravel bed, still as glass, unruffled by any wind, and if, when you paddle in the sea, part of the fascination is the swirls of sand that rise with every step to circle your ankles, here, above close-cut grass, the water was crystal and no footstep could muddy it.

When it was deep enough for Cobweb to swim in, his paws could be seen working underwater as clearly as if he were running in the reflected sky.

Julia called to Libby to tell her she could come in and take off her clothes to be quite at her ease. "Nothing," she said, "makes your clothes so wet as paddling, and the more you hold them up, the wetter they seem to get." So out came Libby, wearing nothing but her nymph's bead.

The cherry trees rose out of a mirror, where the pale undersides of their leaves were reflected upside down. As the flood crept up, getting ever nearer the house, the pansy bed edged with Cobweb's stones was seen perfect underneath, the flowers not bedraggled as when you pick them up out of water, but spread out and as it were dandled by the water. Flagged paths could be followed on the bottom between irises and hart's-tongue ferns. Libby walked along, and the underwater garden swayed at each side as she passed.

One side of the garden was built up in low stone terraces. Here, when she sat half submerged on the lowest wall, from above her head sprawling roses leaned down heavy with flowers. She saw them mirrored all round her, level with her waist, while petals shook down on her and lay on the invisible water, each on its own reflection. Of course, she thought, a garden where everything is reflected is exactly twice as beautiful. And very queer, too, for the fish seemed to be birds. But that of course was only their darting reflections. As for a bathing pool that is the whole garden, with daisies on the bottom that you can pick with your toes and meadowsweet at the edge, no nymph could want more. As she sat on her stone ledge and looked at herself in the water, while her green bead swung forward on its thread and almost touched its double, she suddenly noticed below, down by her feet, some dark glossy leaves which floated outward as she moved her hand, to reveal a cluster of tiny scarlet strawberries. She discovered that they were growing all along the lowest edge of the terrace in the cracks of the flagged path. She hurried to tell Julia this exciting news. Cobweb had long since grown tired of swimming after her and had retired to the dry ground in front of the house, where he sat keeping an eye on things.

"Wild strawberries!" said Julia. "Yes, let's have them for tea. What shall I give you to collect them in?"

She was painting and looked round for some-

thing that would do without her having to move. She picked up off a shelf in the porch a little blue-and-white china basket with a loop handle and china wickerwork with real holes in it. "Just the thing," she said.

The sun was hot on Libby's bare back as she bent down, plunging her arms in above the elbow to catch the fairy strawberries. She filled her basket, working her way along away from the house. If she dipped her basket in and then held it up, a fountain ran out of it all round in a pattern. Whenever she straightened up, she looked round at the extraordinary scene, which was real even if it seemed like a fairy tale.

She had grown so used to the noise of the river that she only remembered now and again to hear it. It pelted along at the other side of the walled bank and seemed too violent to have anything to do with the dream pleasures inside.

By now the house, though still a flight of steps above the water, was itself reflected, exact and beautiful in the long light of afternoon, but it wobbled and broke up as Libby ran out, suddenly keen for her tea and the comfortable privacy of clothes. It was hot on the steps. The strawberries were drained and put to dry in the sun to bring out their flavor; then they were eaten with sugar and cream and lots of scones.

"Did you go up onto the riverbank to see if that crack was widening?" Julia asked as she stretched her arms and legs in a basket chair.

"No," said Libby, and added with shame, "The river frightens me."

"That won't do! Are you afraid of everything that you can't order about? You'll grow up to sit on committees if you're not careful. What I most like about the Babble is that it is the boss round here. It does what it does. It's nice to have something that wasn't thought up by a committee. After all—think of your afternoon today. No committee would think it was proper behavior for a river. It should stay where it was expected to be and not wet people's gardens. I think I must take you to see more of the Babble. If it doesn't rain any more and the level is falling tomorrow, we will follow it up into the hills and see the waterfalls. I'll come with you now to look at that crack."

This time they kept to the stone causeway. Its slabs were old and crumbly, and the cracks were filled with moss and ferns.

Julia and Libby stood hand in hand on the bank. The jostling water, pushing like a herd of pigs, was still six inches below the path, but on the far side where there was no dike, it had covered a long meadow and was taking a ridged and rippling shortcut that way to join the main stream farther down.

The crack in the path was wide enough to put a hand down.

"Isn't this, under the tree, where you said there was a nymph pool?"

Julia with her wonderful bright eyes was always looking at something profoundly interesting, though it never seemed to be people. Nevertheless, she was willing to talk about anything.

"I never said it was one. I said it would do for one."

"What would happen to them if the tree fell in?"

"Oh, I expect they have heard the roots creaking. They have ridden off on the stream like a school of dolphins, to find some wide, quiet mill pool where there won't be rocks rolling round over their feet and a current to fight against."

"Do you know that, or are you only teasing?"

"I don't know it. But one is allowed to imagine. There's no rule against it. I love that big tree."

Libby was very sleepy after being between the water and the hot sun for so long.

Before she went to bed, everything outside had changed again, as when a new scene comes on at the theater. As the sun went down, the mist came up. At first it rose like thin gauze over the water, hardly visible. Then it gradually thickened, seemed to be imprisoned in the valley and restless, breaking up into shapes that moved. When the moon came out, it was beautiful but very ghostly. Libby was glad to pull the window curtains close and then her bed curtains and to sleep in a double privacy. Whatever Julia said, real country, if you weren't used to it, was awfully wild.

Libby slept deeply. When she woke, it was marvelously dim inside her tree pattern. She felt like a bird that wakes at first dawn, but when she looked out of her bed, the sun was shining through the window curtains and they were moving in the breeze.

How quickly the sun had gone down at one side of the earth and come up on the other! It was another day—and what now? The light was suggestive of all surprise and therefore irresistible.

She drew the curtains and looked out. It must, she realized, still be early because the sky was pink. The laughing sun lit up what was left of the mist and turned it into a flippant dance of ghosts at play, in and out of the trees, chasing and vanishing. Libby's window looked to the back, so to see the flooded part of the garden, she had to go down the passage to a window seat.

The mist was thicker over the water but brilliant in the sunlight. It trailed across the pink-silver surface or swirled up from it like tossed hair. It was broken up into suggestions of figures where the water, surprisingly, was in movement, sometimes violent enough to tear the mist apart. She would have said a white arm was raised. She would have thought she heard a laugh. But there was Cobweb, at the edge of the water, barking at a cluster of misty shapes. She knew his "You can't catch me" actions, but there was a quivering quickness about him now that meant danger courted and enjoyed.

The fresh morning breeze let out a breath across the garden that carried off with it half the thinning spirals of vapor—and there *they* were, supple and lovely and white, their long hair swirling round them like the fins of Chinese goldfish, their hands and their smiles enticing Cobweb.

Libby hammered with her fists on the window, shouting, "No! No!" then turned and ran through the twists and corners of the house to fight with the front door.

When she reached the garden, the sun had won. Everything was clear and quietly glittering, though the surface of the water still rocked slightly. The last traces of mist were melting away toward the river— going, gone.

Cobweb was cocky and stimulated, but Libby's heart was still pounding, and she snatched him up.

Julia's window was thrown wide open, and she was there leaning out on her elbows.

"Hallo," she said placidly.

"They shan't have Cobweb," said Libby, trembling with indignation.

"Don't spoil his game. Put the poor dog down. You make a fool of him."

"I don't want him to be pulled down to the bottom."

"Don't worry. I know that bark of his. It's not the sound of a dog that's going to let himself be taken in. On his own ground, too. Nerve, wouldn't you say?"

Libby was dumbfounded. Was it to be taken for granted? Or was Julia mocking her? She dared not ask. She still hugged Cobweb, but now for her own comfort. She sank with him into an armchair in the breakfast room, to commune with him. With Cobweb you knew where you were. He was amiable for a while, then jumped down and shook his fur into place to get rid of that stroked feeling.

Libby laughed. "You were right," she said. "He is very independent."

"You are both terrors for getting up early. It's not seven yet. You can help me to get breakfast."

So nothing was going to be said at all. Did that mean it was a secret between them?

"It's a good thing," said Libby to make conversation, "that your house is on a little hill."

"I guess," Julia replied, "that it was once a small island. It has a habit of privacy."

"You have too," Libby heard herself saying pertly, and then blushed in case it was really rude.

Julia looked at her with those highly intelligent but unmoved eyes and said, "Quite so."

Libby accepted the situation. "Are you taking me to see the waterfalls today?"

"I think we can go. It hasn't rained any more and looks like a fine day, so the flood should start going down soon. We must inspect."

They did not have to go far to find out. In the garden Libby could recognize small flowers holding their necks above water which yesterday had been submerged, or a slab of stone whose surface had been level with the flood was now showing the thickness of its side.

"It is down two inches," Julia agreed. "When it is past the peak, it drops very quickly. We must go this morning before the waterfalls are spent. Look at the rate at which it is getting away."

They had gone as far as the riverbank to look at the big tree. There was an eddy under it where the current noisily sucked at the bank, where loops of bare root could be seen. The crack in the footpath was certainly wider. When the light wind passed through the leaves with a playful push, below the usual rustle there was a creaking, somewhere in the trunk.

"It has had many floods before in its long life," said Julia, "only not often with all its leaves on. They say the roots are always as wide as the tree, so it has plenty of anchorage. So long as a strong wind doesn't get up! I imagine that creaking means the roots are hanging on like grim death. Hold up, my beauty," she said, patting the tree as if it were a horse.

Julia packed a picnic, not forgetting Cobweb's preferences, and they set off in the car along the valley. There was a water splash at each side of the bridge, but otherwise the way was clear. A single-track road meandered along, mostly beside the river, but often taking a wide swoop to serve a solitary farm. All the way, on both sides, the country had that exhilarating confidence and freshness that had so surprised Libby on her first morning. They parked the car in a farmyard and set off on foot. Almost every step brought a new scent, spicy if it was bracken or yew or wild rose, drowsy if it was mountain ash or meadowsweet. Even stone, she discovered, has a smell, and a dell of boulders covered with moss and ferns down which moisture dripped had the strangest smell of all.

They had left the car at a point where the main valley divided into two. These narrower, steeper clefts went up and back till they were lost in the hilltops, and down each came a leaping stream, shouting as it came. The hillsides were streaked with silver threads, each of which was a brooklet running down to join the rest, and each of these, if you were near enough to hear, had a voice like ducklings hurrying after their mother.

At the junction where the two main streams met, it was a tussle of tearing rapids, not exactly a waterfall. It was as if each torrent had collected on its way the roar re-echoing in its rocky and confined course and had then poured the double volume in a cataract of triumphant din. There was so much energy, purpose, and delight in this meeting and forward rush of water that Libby found it impossible not to think of the river as alive. Cobweb treated it as a friend. He drank from the edge and ran about with his ears cocked, very much on tiptoe and alert.

Julia and Libby began to climb the hillside. There was a track through the woods such as woodcutters in Grimms' tales might have made. The sound of the water was muffled by the trees, and its dewy smell lost in the far stronger smell of leaves and loam, which suggests animals and their lairs. The crackling of their footsteps was an intrusion into a great privacy. The calls of tits and blackbirds warned the wood of strangers.

They came out of the trees onto a rocky mound, high above the river, where its noise came up to them again, vibrating over the whole valley. From this point they could see three waterfalls, one behind the other up the hillside. The nearest and far the largest was a sheer drop over an overhanging cliff. Imagine a big incoming wave finding no shore to break on, but falling and falling. At the bottom was a rocky basin into which the continuous water plunged with a drumming like pistons, or like the throb of a terrifying heart. Libby put her hands over her ears, but Julia was shouting to her.

"You see how the water falls clear of the cliff. You can walk underneath the fall if you like. There's a path cut in the rock along a ledge. You'd be quite dry. There's a cave, too, but that is rather trickly."

"How, tricky?"

"Trickly, wet."

"Who would cut a path there?"

"I don't know. Perhaps shepherds, or hunters. It does instead of a bridge. There's not as much water usually. This is the result of a cloudburst. I often take Cobweb over—but look at him now—his legs are trembling."

Libby found that hers were, too. She shook her head, and they started climbing again. As they got higher up, they could, in clearances between the trees,

look back at the course of the Babble down their own valley and beyond.

"There's a lot of poetry about every river coming at last to the sea, but it's always very sordid and sad when they get there, and long before that everyone throws rubbish and lets drains into them. Once people offered sacrifices to rivers," said Julia. "I think that was better."

The second and smaller waterfall was in every way different. No two could possibly be alike. Its fall was not precipitous but broken by jutting rocks of all shapes and sizes. Over these the water was broken into star shapes or jets and flung out so much spray that in the sun it was like a firework display with drops instead of sparks. All these sprays fell back into the cataract from different heights and angles, making a varied and most musical sound. Libby could have listened to it for hours and could not be dragged away, so they decided to have their picnic there, sitting on the turf with their backs to comfortable boulders.

The sky was high and blue. The pearly clouds sailed across, changing shape as Libby watched. Under them the hills rose and fell, seeming as though they also changed their shape as the cloud shadows passed up and down them. Libby hardly knew whether to think it was always different or always the same. The earth was warm under her, alive with grasshoppers and wild bees, and the wagtails, running, flicking, and bobbing, were around as well. Libby's thoughts ran here and there with them.

"Are there waterfall spirits?" she asked.

"Perhaps. I've heard of mountain spirits, called oriads."

"What do they do?"

"Who knows? Perhaps, if they approve of you, they guide you through the mist; or, if you are wondering how you could make money out of the mountain with quarries or timber-felling, they push you over the waterfall. What would you think?"

"Where do they live? In caves?"

"Oh yes, surely! That one underneath the waterfall. Generally the water is only a light glittering curtain, just enough to make the cave private. And however much they chattered in there, the river would drown it. You might think you heard them, but you'd never be sure."

Libby listened even more carefully and looked round to be sure she knew her way back.

Cobweb was sitting up at attention, his whiskers twitching and his eyes shut to help him to catch the scent. Julia, bending to look where his muzzle was pointing, nudged Libby from her daydream and said, "Look!"

Across the valley, not too far to be clearly seen, a patch of bracken ended on a ridge, below which were scattered boulders. Among these, in and out of the shadows, five tiny fox cubs were playing and tumbling, while their mother lay sleepily snapping at flies. She was probably perfectly aware of Cobweb, but the ravine at the bottom of which ran the river with its rising cloud of vapor and commotion was between them.

Before long the leading edges of the clouds began to tatter and wave in front of them, like the hair of people with their backs to the wind. They hustled along, streaming endlessly up from behind the hill that sheltered the picnickers.

"There's wind up there," said Julia. "The clouds aren't being allowed to dilly-dally. Let's go up a little higher."

They climbed again, frequently jumping over those duckling-voiced brooklets that fumbled their way down through the rough grass.

The third waterfall seemed to spring young and gay over the skyline. It dived lightly from pool to pool and zigzagged between them as careless as a butterfly. If the second fall had been unfrequented, this one was absolutely solitary. Its flashing and splashing was for the sky alone. But for its voice, the silence was profound and disquieting.

Libby by now believed in every kind of spirit, of rock, air, wind, water, and tree, also in others who might appear as wolf, toad, sheep, or owl. She was abashed and had had enough.

It was quicker and easier going home downhill, racing in curves round boulders or checking one's too sudden speed by clutching a tree. The wind followed them down and made the trees throw up their hands in protest.

As they drove back along the lower reaches, Libby remembered what the valley had looked like from up the hillside. The long racecourse of the river seemed to go right through her. Now that she knew

it better, she understood that the Babble really was the lord of the valley.

They reached home in the early evening, and already it seemed home to Libby after the solitudes in which she had been. The trees in the garden, familiar yet mysterious, lifted their spreading branches as the wind passed, as if they breathed deeply. They rustled, each one individually, whispering and murmuring under their breath. They were stable and comfortable things to come back to. Unlike the river, they stayed for you. The larks sang, coming down now, not climbing, a contented homing song, and the other birds were telling, each in his own way, of the day coming to an end.

Julia and Libby had been away ten hours. During their absence the water had retreated from the garden. The enchanted lake of the nymphs had vanished into the river, as they had themselves. The Babble's whim had taken one day to come, had lasted one wonderful day and night, and now was gone again. The garden was as wet as anyone would be after an immersion, but tomorrow no one would know what dreams and fancies the Babble could bring about.

Julia was longing for tea, and Libby hungry and tired. They were anxious to see how the tree on the bank was doing, but that must wait. Cobweb curled himself on the sofa and went to sleep, his breath stirring the hair of his ribs. Libby ate in silence, lying relaxed in an armchair, thinking perhaps of the foxes, perhaps of the strange beliefs and fears that she had found she had, perhaps just of the skyey solitude up there.

Presently the window curtain fluttered inward and flicked the sugar tongs off the table.

"The wind's getting up," said Julia, rousing herself to close the window. "I am going to see how far the river has gone down and what my tree looks like."

Libby and Cobweb jumped up, too, and they all went out, crossing the causeway in single file because the grass was still marshy.

The Babble was dashing along, emptying itself as fast as it could. The level of water had dropped surprisingly, so that it was possible to see how far it had eaten under the bank. Libby cried out when she saw the crack in the footpath, now wide enough to put her arm down if she had dared. By some optical illusion—perhaps caused by the water rushing by—the ground between the crack and the edge seemed to move outward, so that Libby kept nervously on the inside of the path. The fresh wind tossed the branches and turned the leaves upside down so that they twittered shrilly. Somewhere in the trunk there was an unhealthy creaking. Libby was sure she saw the trunk itself sway just visibly, while up through the crack in the path came a sound of displaced gravel slipping down.

The wind ceased; the twigs and leaves steadied themselves and grew still. The tree held its long-established place in the air, in the view. A swallow perched on the branch it habitually chose and twittered on and on. Then it flashed away to pick up flies. Another rougher gust blew, during which the tree lurched and righted itself unsteadily with a sound like the creaking of ropes. From underground came a series of sharp snappings, and the crack wriggled like a snake on the path.

"Where's Cobweb?" said Julia.

Cobweb was halfway back to the house watching with his tail between his legs. Libby felt the wind hit the back of her neck, and the tree seemed to throw up its arms with what can only be thought of as a scream; the branches swayed wildly and clashed together, the ground heaved, and the tree fell backward like someone pushed off a pier. It hit the water with a gigantic smack, sending a tidal wave downstream while the sky rained with the splash. Then some of its drowned arms sprang up out of the river throwing water around. Instantly the river, half dammed, began snarling and foaming among the submerged branches, tearing off the leaves and roaring its frustration. Broken boughs went sailing off downstream or lodged themselves against the trunk and made the blockage worse. The roots stuck up vertically like the spokes of a cartwheel, half the footpath clinging to them. The swallow, swooping back to find its perch, had to complete its circle in empty air. The other birds that had fled at the crash came back calling to each other in surprise or distress at the unexpected emptiness, for nests had gone over with the tree, spilling out their blue eggs.

Libby had gone white, and her fingers were

spread out stiff with excitement. Julia sighed deeply.

"The moon will never shine on it again," she said.

There was a moon that night, though it rose late. Libby could not get properly to sleep; dreams and waking were hopelessly mixed. Now it was the pounding of the waterfall, now the screech and rattle of the tree that kept her awake, then it would be her tree-patterned bed in which faces looked out at her whichever way she turned, till the whole thing collapsed on top of her. This was really a dream—she was tied up in the bedclothes. The moon was shining so brightly through the French window that the curtains were seen as trees against the light.

Libby got out of bed to look at the garden. How beautiful the trees were with the moon shining on their heads! She knew now what Julia meant. Kings and queens standing there with tremendous dignity.

The wind was making a sad other-worldly sound, a perpetual passing-by, in which there was an undertone of sobbing, and presently she heard the softest possible fluted wail from Cobweb, as if in sympathy.

"Cobweb," she called, bending and putting her hand down for him. But what she felt was cool, tremulous skin and heavy hair sliding over shoulders, and what she then saw in the moonlight at her feet was a girl huddled on the ground.

Libby put consoling arms round her and turned the desolate face up to the moon. She knew it at once. Cobweb was licking her feet.

"You are crying because you have lost your tree. It was a special beauty, I know, and your own, and

the moon will never shine on it again. But don't cry."

She went on murmuring everything comforting she could think of, while she coaxed the sobbing thing into her bed among the leafy folds. "Don't cry. It's a special bed for dryads, a halfway house till you find another tree. Look. I'll pull all the curtains close. It's a tree house." Even so, the moon shone faintly through and showed against the white sheets the dusky body and the tumbled dark hair. Libby brought her brush and comb and sat with her, soothingly brushing down the long strands, rhythmically again and again, till the lovely creature was covered with sleek ordered tresses, smooth as beech leaves, and she slept, and Libby with her.

"Wake up, Libby! Wake up, wake up."

It was Julia standing by her bed.

"Wake up."

Libby looked wildly round, but she was alone, except for Julia watching her, her eyes bright like some noble legendary animal's that one might find looking at one, on waking up in a forest.

"My brother has arrived earlier than I expected, and we are having breakfast."

Libby struggled to get her ideas the right way up. The sun had taken the place of the moon; otherwise, nothing looked different in her room. The French window was still open.

"Where's Cobweb?" she asked.

"Oh, he'll never leave Charles now he's back. Are you properly awake? Have you forgotten that I

must take you home today? Hurry then, my dear. It's late. Why, you funny girl, you've been sleeping on your hairbrush!"

Julia picked up the brush and saw on it a long dark-green hair. She slid it through her fingers thoughtfully and said nothing.

At breakfast, in the presence of a large unknown man, Libby thought that perhaps saying nothing was the right way. Certainly it was the easiest. Julia and he were discussing how to get a gang of men to clear away the fallen tree out of the river, so that Libby was free to think her own thoughts. She liked men. She was fascinated by their bulk, their differentness, and their lordly smiles that were more indulgent than women's.

When Julia was out of the room telephoning, Charles and Libby sat opposite each other in mutual curiosity. Cobweb was sitting on Charles's knee with the superior look of a dog who has a man.

"My sister tells me," said Charles, "that you are one of the lucky ones."

Libby was startled, in case he might be referring to what they were not talking about. She looked at him anxiously, but decided she might trust him with a careful question or two.

"The trees in your garden, I suppose, are very old?" she began.

"Old," he replied, "but still in their prime."

"I should guess," she ventured further, "that *if* there were dryads, if they were true, those trees, as they are so special, would be occupied?"

"Very likely," he replied gravely.

"Is there a new tree that might do?"

He considered for a while, saying half to himself, "Not too large, not too small, not so newly planted that it hasn't taken firm hold. Yes, I think we have one. Come over here a minute."

Libby came, obedient and mystified. He measured her skinny waist between his hands.

"Just about right, I should think. Come along and I'll show you. It's a lime. I put it in two years ago. They live a very long time."

It was a perfect young tree, its trunk just about the same as Libby's waist, its spread of shade enough for one, its head rounded enough for the moon to gild. Libby sat with her back against the trunk hugging her knees and looking up through the branches. It was in flower and smelled very sweet. The bees up there filled the air with a sleepy, floating drone.

"That's just right," she said, and ran off into the house.

When Charles came back later after a walk with Cobweb, he paused by the tree. There was a drawing pin stuck in the bark, from which hung a loose tassel of long green hair. There was also a tiny stick-on label saying "Reserved." Cobweb lay down in its shade and rubbed the side of his face on the bark.

Charles went on to the house where he could hear Julia and Libby packing.

"I hadn't forgotten I was going today," said Libby. "I just couldn't bear to think about it. I don't feel I can bear it."

"We always feel like that when we leave here," said Charles. "Come with me and say good-bye to the Babble."

They went off together across the warm, dry garden, where flowers were sunning themselves in the cracks of stone paths and the rose bushes leaned over but found no mirror.

Across the river from side to side lay the up-rooted tree, now a bridge instead of a dam, for the water had sunk back to its usual summer level and was laughing over its stone bed as when Libby had first seen it. Cobweb was fishing for mouth-sized stones.

"Such a lot has happened and unhappened since I came," said Libby.

Much later, with the seemingly endless car journey behind her, she jumped out into her mother's arms and was hugged and kissed.

"Have you had a lovely time? Tell me all about it. I want to hear everything."

Why is it that when one comes back after a totally enthralling adventure, there is so little one can say about it? Libby gazed at her mother, big-eyed, her head seething with excitement. "There were—" she began, helter-skelter, then hesitated. She tried again. "There was—" She stopped regretfully.

"What was there, darling? I can see it was special."

"There was a dog called Cobweb," she finally got out, as if that meant everything. But all the rest had become private.